APOCALYPSE BOW WOW

APOCALYPSE BOW WOW

James Proimos III

illustrated by
James Proimos Jr.

BLOOMSBURY
LONDON NEW DELHI NEW YORK SYDNEY

Bloomsbury Publishing, London, New Delhi, New York and Sydney

First published in Great Britain in January 2015 by Bloomsbury Publishing Plc
50 Bedford Square, London WC1B 3DP

First published in the USA in January 2015 by
Bloomsbury Children's Books
1385 Broadway, New York, New York 10018

www.bloomsbury.com

Bloomsbury is a registered trademark of Bloomsbury Publishing Plc

A CIP catalogue record for this book is available from the British Library

ISBN 978 1 4088 5498 3

Printed and bound in Great Britain by CPI Group (UK) Ltd, Croydon CR0 4YY

1 3 5 7 9 10 8 6 4 2

For Apollo and Brownie

The Prologue

Outside, something terribly strange was happening.

Clothes lines were ablaze.

Humans had vanished from moving cars.

And ancient texts began to rumble.

Scene
One

It just means I am better than you because they know who my parents are.

Hmph. Well, they rescued me from that place with the bars.

I think that means they like me more.

It means you were free! The man must have got you. He's a cheapo.

Scene
Two

14

17

Scene
Three

Scene
Four

23

24

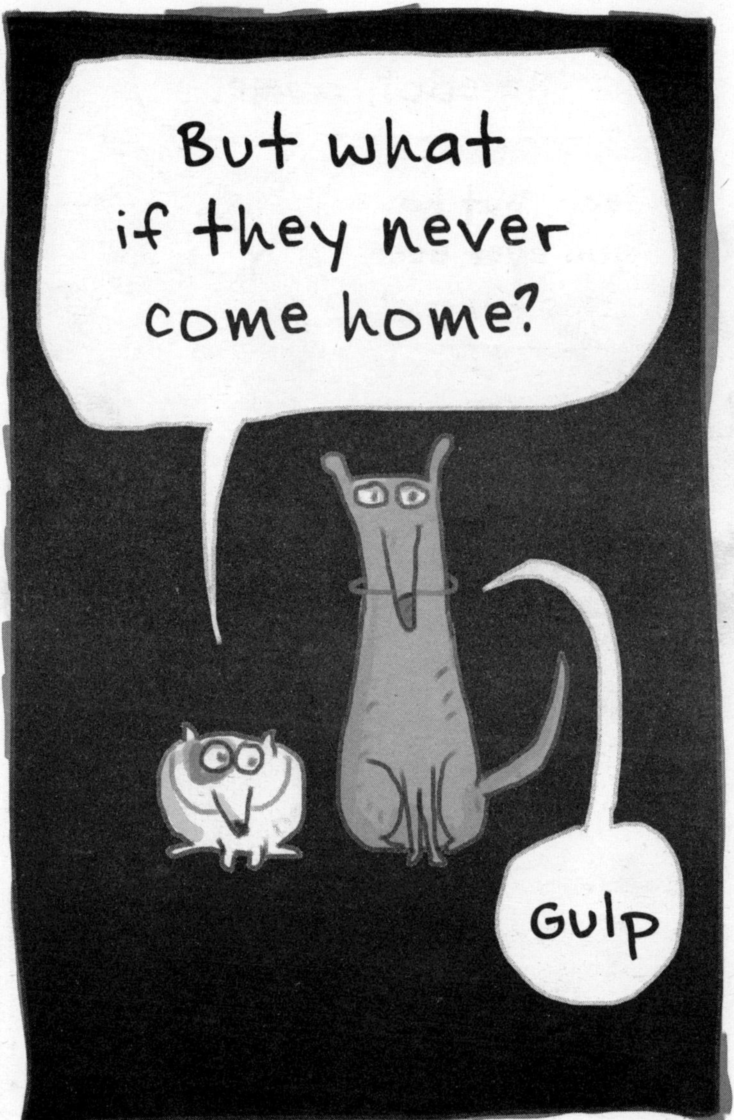
But what if they never come home?
Gulp

Scene
Five

28

29

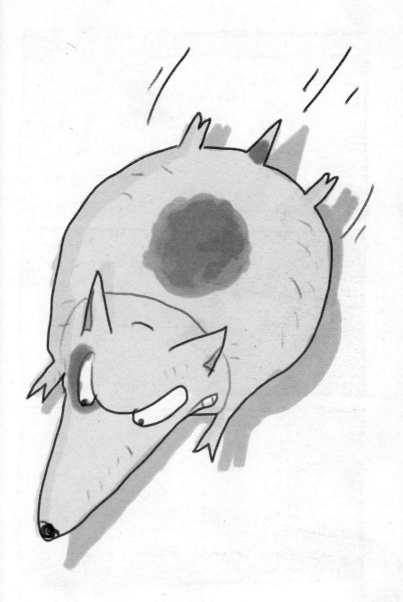

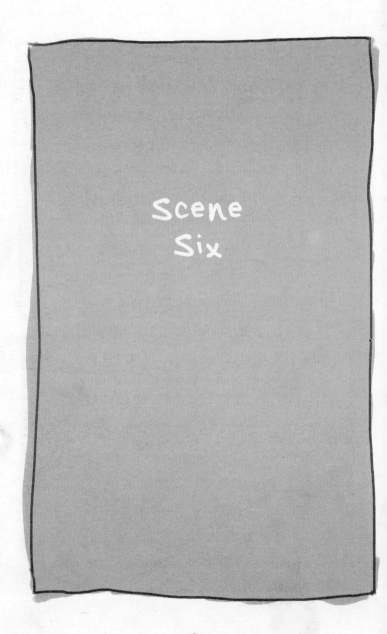

Scene
Six

36

40

41

43

46.

48

Scene
Seven

54

55

The only advice I have is to try the supermarket. Usually there are lots of people there.

Super-market?

That big building full of food.

Scene
Eight

Scene
Nine

73

Scene
Ten

Scene
Eleven

83

85

Scene
Twelve

I told them there was a whole bunch of tough dogs here. They have no idea it is only us.
Hee, hee.

Scene
Thirteen

Scene
Fourteen

99

Let me tell you both something that might make you think twice about continuing this good dog/tiny dog routine. I am FERAL!

104

III

112

Interval

What the rat found when he finally awoke from his nap was that an alliance had been formed. The law dog was to be their leader. And "helpers" would be allowed to join the "team" so that a small army could be formed to protect their new home from those who might want to steal their food.

That was some nap!

Scene
Fifteen

Hours
Later

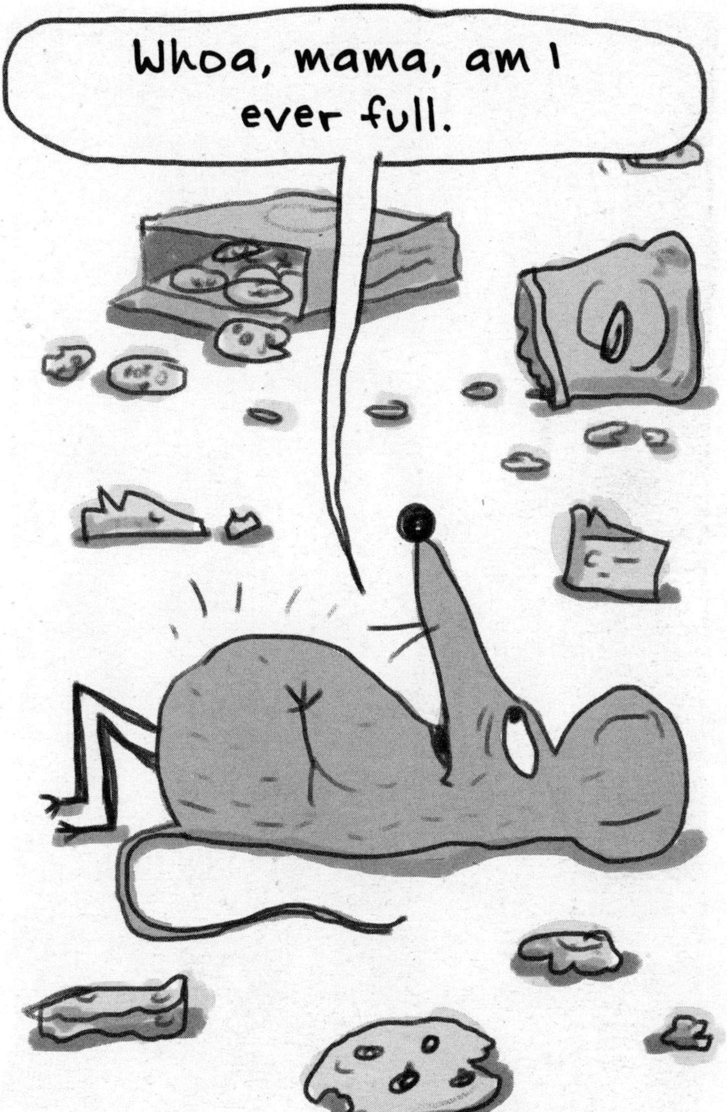
Whoa, mama, am I ever full.

Scene
Sixteen

133

Scene
Seventeen

137

Scene
Eighteen

Tell your pals that tomorrow at the stroke of midnight, we are taking over this place!

And if you care for your well-being, you'll be outta the joint!

Scene
Nineteen

Scene
Twenty

153

156

157

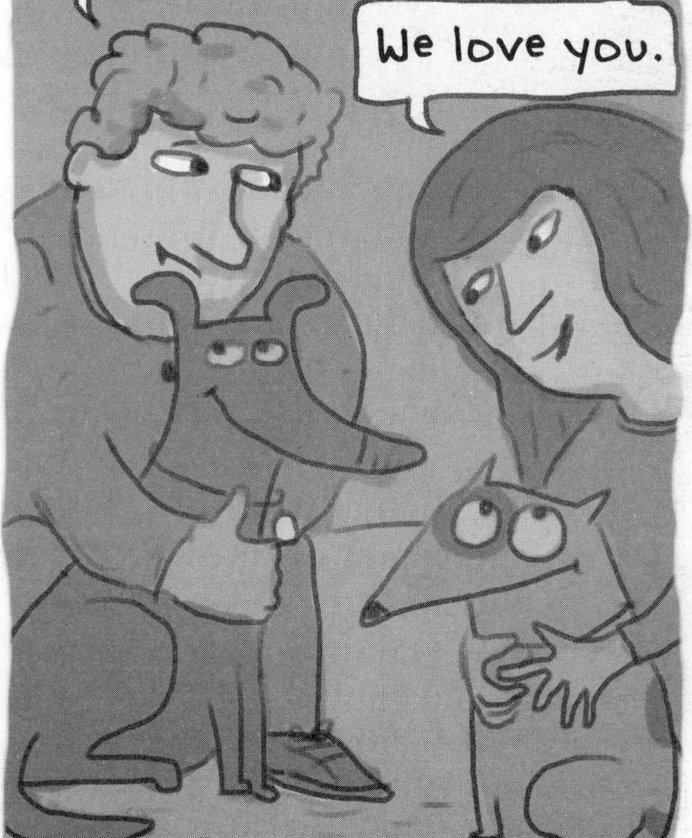
We are going to take you home now.
We love you.

Scene Twenty-one: The Battle

OUCH! POW!

The battle
started out badly
for our heroes.
But suddenly, the
silly dog began
giving brilliant and
timely fighting
advice to each
one of his friends.

BAM! WONK! UGH!

Scene Twenty-two: The Cop

Scene Twenty-three: The Boss

Scene Twenty-four: The Rat

185

186

Scene
Twenty-five:
The Angry One

The opportunity of defeating the enemy is provided by the enemy himself.

Scene
Twenty-six:
The Kitty

193

Scene Twenty-seven: The Battle Turns

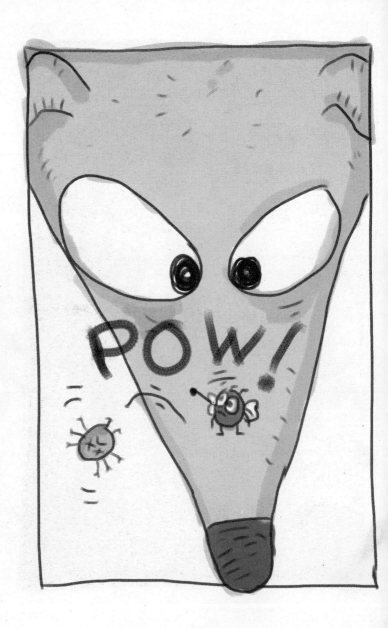

Scene Twenty-eight: The Escape

Scene
Twenty-nine

207

208

Scene
Thirty

210

214

To be
continued . . .

LOOK OUT FOR

APOCALYPSE
MIAOW MIAOW

COMING SOON . . .